This book belongs to:

_____

A Lost Star Named Stella

By Jackie Perucki
Illustrated by Larisa Ivankovic

Starkeeper Publishing
Columbus, Ohio

Library of Congress Control Number: 2020923556

Paperback ISBN: 978-0-578-81114-7
Hardcover ISBN: 978-0-578-82436-9
Kindle ASIN: B08QCG4BBZ

For Natalie

Lift up your eyes and look to the heavens:
Who created all these?

He who brings out the starry host one by one
and calls forth each of them by name.
Because of His great power and mighty strength,
not one of them is missing.
Isaiah 40:26

Have you ever looked up at the night sky?
Full of shining and twinkling stars?
Did you know every star has a name?
Maybe one has the same name as yours!

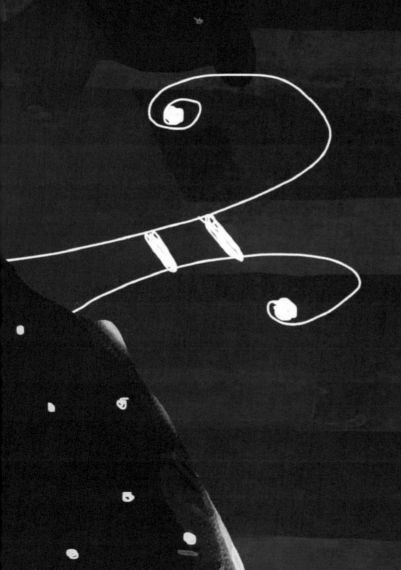

One sweet little star was named Stella.
She glittered, glistened, and gleamed.
She always lit up the sky in the same place,
Until one night she got lost while you dreamed.

It's quite easy for stars to get lost,

For it's dark out at nighttime, you know.

Since stars have names, they have feelings too-

And poor Stella felt afraid and alone.

She wandered around 'til she met the moon.

"I can't help, I am busy," he said.

Stella went on 'til she met the sun,
But she just told her to go back to bed.

She waved at a comet, asking for help,
But it sped up and passed her on by.

Giving up, she sat down, right where she was,
And with that, Stella started to cry.

She was just about to fall fast asleep,
When she felt a warm hand on her own.
Who could that be? Stella thought to herself,
And she hoped that her tears wouldn't show.

The Bright Morning Star stood beaming so bright,
That he dried every tear with His glow.
"Stella," He said, with a clear, calming voice,
"I will show you the way you should go."

Then He took her hand and He led her north-
To the place where her family glimmered.
Stella joined them again, no longer lost,
And they smiled at how brightly she shimmered.

Now, children, like stars, who have lost their way,

May find it hard to get back on their own.

But you'll find your path, if you follow Him –

He who leads all the stars to their homes.

The End

For God so loved the world that He gave His one and only Son, that whoever believes in him shall not perish but have eternal life.   John 3:16

CPSIA information can be obtained
at www.ICGtesting.com
Printed in the USA
LVHW071725080321
680884LV00001B/7